This edition published 2012 for Index Books
Published by Top That! Publishing plc
Tide Mill Way, Woodbridge, Suffolk, IP12 1AP, UK
www.topthatpublishing.com
Text copyright © Jaclin Azoulay 2011
All rights reserved
0 2 4 6 8 9 7 5 3 1
Printed and bound in China

Creative Director – Simon Couchman
Editorial Director – Daniel Graham

Written by Jaclin Azoulay
Illustrated by The Fénix Factory

ISBN 978-1-84956-303-1

A catalogue record for this book is available from the British Library
Printed and bound in China

Hic!

Written by Jaclin Azoulay

For my mum Pat, my dad Angelo, my Uncle Owen,
Raz, Inbar, Gai, Daniel, Lia and Oded. With love always.

Snuffletrump the piglet was sad.
Everyone seemed to have forgotten it was
his birthday today. No cards, no presents,
just ... '**Hic!**' – the hiccups.

Mummy Pig and Daddy
Pig were very busy.
When Snuffletrump asked
if he could help, all that
came out was, '**Hic!**'
'Oink! You go off and play!'
Daddy Pig told Snuffletrump.

But Snuffletrump was too sad to play, '**Hic!**', so he went to visit Cow instead. When Cow heard Snuffletrump's hiccups she said, 'Goodness moo!'

Cow told Snuffletrump that the only cure for
hiccups was to drink a glass of her milk ...

... whilst standing on your head.
But it didn't help. '**Hic!**'

Poor Snuffletrump! Now he had the hiccups, no happy birthday, and milk all over him!
'**Hic!** Thank you for trying to help, Cow,' he said.

Over at the hen house the naughty, pecky, gossipy hens laughed, 'Bok, bok, bok, bok, bok!' when they heard Snuffletrump's hiccups. '**Hic!**'

'Everyone knows what you cock-a-doodle-do to cure the hiccups!' said Rooster, with a glint in his eye. 'You must juggle some eggs!'

Snuffletrump wasn't so sure, but he didn't want to be rude. He started to juggle the eggs. Splat! Splat! Splat! '**Hic!**' Snuffletrump now had hiccups, no happy birthday, milk all down his face, and egg on his head too!

Snuffletrump didn't feel like saying anything to those mean old hens, but he remembered his manners.
'**Hic!** Thank you for trying to help,' he said.

Snuffletrump sat down feeling very sad and alone.
'Mummy Pig! Daddy Pig!' he cried. 'I feel like a pancake!
Hic!' He looked all around, but poor Snuffletrump
couldn't see Mummy Pig or Daddy Pig anywhere.

Horse whinnied to Snuffletrump from the field. Snuffletrump trotted over, '**Hic!**'

'Don't worry!' said Horse. 'The best cure for hiccups is a good old jiggetty-jog. Climb up onto my back!'

Snuffletrump sat on Horse's back and they jigged and jogged and bumped and bounced all around the field.

It was wonderful fun ...

... until Horse saw Mole poke his head up and stopped in surprise. Poor Snuffletrump was catapulted through the air. 'Wheee! **Hic!**'

'Thank you for trying to help, Horse,'
Snuffletrump said. 'But now I have
hiccups, no happy birthday, milk all
down my face, egg on my head, and
straw stuck everywhere! **Hic!**'

Duck quacked at Snuffletrump from the pond, where she was teaching her ducklings to swim.
'Oh, Snuffletrump!' she said. 'I heard your hiccups from over here! You frightened my ducklings! Quack!'
'Sorry, Duck. **Hic!**' said Snuffletrump.

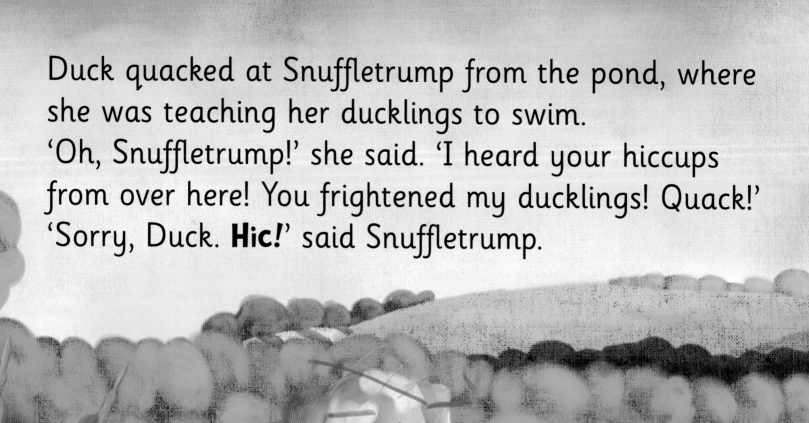

'Don't you know that the surest cure for
hiccups is a splash of cold water?' Duck said.
With that, Duck and all of her ducklings started
splishing and splashing Snuffletrump.

When they had stopped splashing, Snuffletrump
stood and waited. Duck and her ducklings waited.
'Oh!' Snuffletrump said, at last, with a smile.
'I'm clean again! Thank you Duck, thank you ducklings!
My hiccups have ...

Hic! ... still not gone.'
Snuffletrump was clean, but he still had no happy birthday, and he still had the hiccups!

Then Snuffletrump saw Mummy Pig and Daddy Pig waving to him from the barn, so he headed over there as fast as he could.

'HAPPY BIRTHDAY SNUFFLETRUMP!'
Mummy Pig and Daddy Pig and all of
Snuffletrump's friends were in the barn with the
biggest birthday party he had ever seen!

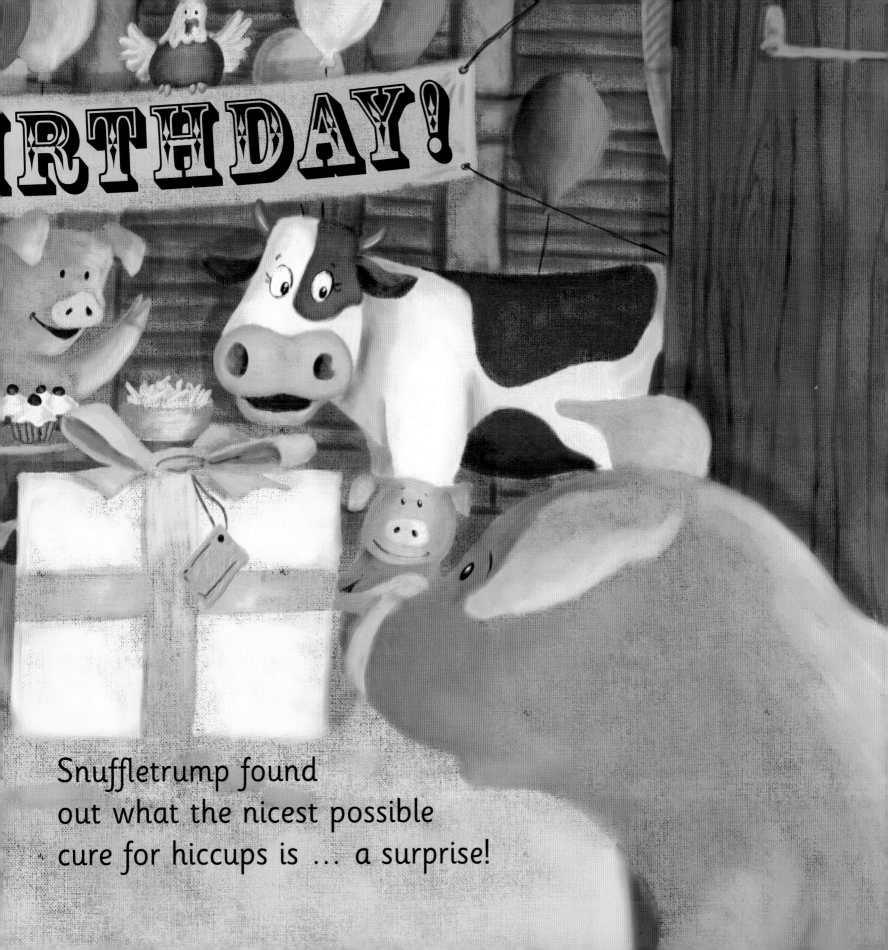

Snuffletrump found
out what the nicest possible
cure for hiccups is ... a surprise!

More great picture books from Top That! Publishing

ISBN 978-1-84956-303-1

Snuffletrump the piglet will try
anything to get rid of his hiccups!

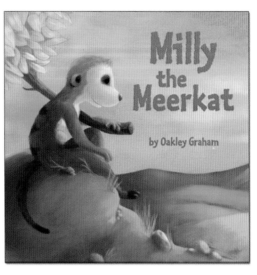

ISBN 978-1-84956-304-8

Milly the meerkat learns a very
important lesson in this classic tale.

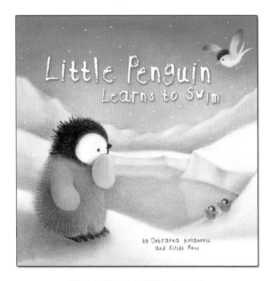

ISBN 978-1-84956-440-3

Little Penguin learns to overcome
his fears with help from his friends.

ISBN 978-1-84956-305-5

The animals are making a hullabaloo
in this humorous picture storybook!